All Things in Moderation

A Collection of Stories and Poems
Volume I

Virginia Joyann "Jody" Haley Smith

Gina McKnight, Editor

Monday Creek Publishing
Ohio USA

On the Front Cover:
Top Left: Jody's High School Graduation Portrait
Top Right: Jody astride Wayne Smith's Arabian, Colorado
Bottom Left: Jody with Puff, 1976 AKC National Specialty Best of
Winners with her beloved Belgian Sheepdog, The Magic Dragon V
Siegestor CD/TD, "Puff
Bottom Right: Jody crossing the Hocking River riding New Forest Pony,
Junco, at Hocking College's National Trail Horse Challenge

Monday Creek Publishing | P.O. Box 399 | Buchtel, Ohio USA
mondaycreekpublishing.com

1. Smith, Virginia Joyann "Jody" Smith 2. Short Stories 3. Poetry 4. Essays

ISBN-10: 979-8-9860490-9-0

For
Pat and Jessica

Contents

Foreword

My grandmother — equal parts strong, stubborn, resilient — was the matriarch of my family. Jody could be found weekly on summer evenings in a camp chair with a dog of choice outside of Ohio University's Memorial Auditorium enjoying the free concerts on the College Green.

Jody would frequently go to the West State Street Dog Park followed by a short trip to Larry's Dawghouse, Athens, Ohio, where she would take advantage of her senior dis-count on Weenie Wednesdays with her usual order of a raspberry ice-cream soda and regular hot dog with everything but pickles. Without fail, her grandchildren could al-ways count on seeing her in her proud Federal Hocking grandparent hoodie (...ironically, I went to Athens) sitting in the stands of our football, basketball, baseball, soccer and swimming competitions. She walked faster than her grandsons despite being nearly a foot shorter in stature.

Her competitive nature extended to the animals she cared for so diligently. The individual accomplishments she was most proud of were her top four finishes in numerous trail riding competitions and winning AKC "Best of Breed" with Puff, her beloved Belgian Sheepdog.

Jody's love for animals served as a refuge for her: Acknowledging that their love was built conditionally, she knew it was pure, constant, and could be counted on in times of difficulty with personal relationships. In such times, she put her energy into caring for the variety of animals at Milliron Farm. During these points in her life, she turned away from writing, returning to creative expression when she felt a greater sense of stability.

Jody's reverence for the written word tied in with her spirituality. She believed in words as a pathway to greater connection with self, and she kept a careworn Bible on her bedside table, its pages faded to yellow from years of perusal in times of duress. She wrote Letters to the Editor of the local paper in abundance. For her, the collaborative nature of the editing process created the opportunity to delve into another's perspective, allowing a glimmer into a reality divergent from her own.

Honoring that connection to language, I'll share a memory of Grandma Jody that I feel speaks to the nature of her personality. July of 2011 was a sweat-soaked month, temperatures easily topping 100 degrees. It'd just reached double digits, and the Athens County fair was weeks away. While training my dog, Skipper, to win the novice category in the dog obedience competition, I planned to live with Grandma Jody for a few weeks (she was unparalleled in her ability to connect with animals). She drove Skipper and I to the vet clinic before we walked over the cattle guard at the base of her driveway together. There, we embarked on our first challenge: a race up the steep, gravel drive-way leading to her house. The only rule: you couldn't run. Fast walking, jumping, skip-ping, and even crawling were permitted. Skipper took an early lead up the first half, capitalizing on his freedom to ignore the rules set for the humans. Being a dark, triple coated Australian shepherd in the mid-July heat, he quickly fell behind his pack. Worried for my dog, I stopped as I was about to pass him to give him a pet and check if he was okay. (He was). This was the opportunity Jody was looking for - she didn't wait for opportunities - and she surged past us to reach the towering white oak at the top of her driveway, thereby earning bragging rights over her grandson 62 years her junior. While Skipper padded over to the house looking for a grassy bit of shade, Jody first hugged and then proceeded to kiss the oak tree and asked me to do the same. Despite the fact that we were alone, as well as my prior knowledge of this custom, I blushed with embarrassment.

Eventually, I relented, placing my lips to the bark. She was grandma, after all, and she had beat me fair and square. Until that tree fell in a derecho, I always kissed that oak when I walked to the top of her driveway.

Now ten years later, when asked to introduce this collection of writings by Jody Smith, I am at a loss for words to explain how or why she authored these writings. I do enjoy the thought that she was not much older than I am now. Although her life's circumstances were much different from mine, it is a gift to read her thoughts and stories from her young life.

Noah Franklin Fox
August 11, 2022

Introduction

A scholar in every way, Jody Smith was a prolific writer. Her stories and poems tell of her childhood, family, pets, and marriage. Born in Toledo, raised in Mansfield, she excelled through school and college. She majored in English at Colorado State University, earning accolades for academic success.

In this volume, mostly written between 1958-1967, you will find Jody's fictional characters intertwined with true life. *Why I Write* is a reflection of dreams and goals. As a young veterinarian's wife with two children, Jody tells why she enrolled in a correspondence course to propel her writing; *Au Revoir* is the story of a young woman vacationing in Europe. It's her last day in Paris and she is anxious to return home to reconnect with her true love; *More Than One Way to Skin a Cat* is the story of training a young horse to the cart – which was Jody's specialty; *Scarlet Ribbons* reveals Jody's love of horses, the barn, and miracles; *I'm Pooh* was inspired by the family cat – a real cat that was as ornery as portrayed; *Gray Galloper* is a memory of Jody as a young girl roaming the alleyways of her Mansfield neighborhood on her imaginary horse the "Black". Her brother Gary and dog Sport are part of the tale as she becomes infatuated with a carousel horse and hopes to take it home; *Cruising Down the River* is a thrilling ride through flooded river waters, only to find that Jody and her friend are headed for trouble. Jody's love of canoeing and an almost fatal trip over a roaring dam will keep you engaged. This true story was reported in the local newspaper as well as Jody's daily journal; *Impulse* is about home, integrity, tradition, and faith; *The Hunt* takes us into the woods on horseback with Jody and her guide. The day is cold and the deer are hiding just as Jody becomes listless and begins daydreaming of her trip to Rome; *Anticipation* is the story of a girl who is coming-of-age. She reflects on her young life while waiting for her boyfriend. While she waits, she reminisces about the neighbors, the aesthetics of her neighborhood, her trusty canine, and time with horses.

Jody's love for animals is documented here. From an early age she found joy in keeping all sorts of pets. As she matured, her love for horses became paramount. She became a skillful equestrian and kept horses throughout her lifetime, including her beloved gelding Starboy. She was a keeper of sheep, goats, cats, dogs, horses, ducks, and more. Her journals are filled with timetables for vaccinations, deworming, and preventive care. As a dog trainer, she won AKC accolades with Puff, her Belgian Shepherd.

Relocating from Colorado to Ohio, Jody and her veterinarian husband, Abbott P. Smith, built Milliron Clinic and farm. Their historic farmhouse sat on a hill above the clinic. They raised two children, Jessica and Pat, and was proud of their grandchildren, AJ, Grant, and Noah.

Along with Jody's short stories and poetry, we present to you a talented woman who was a fan of Roy Rogers, enjoyed writing, reading, academia, music, and, most of all, loved living in southeastern Ohio.

Gina McKnight

Why I Write

I'm studying writing to escape from the rut of non-thinking busywork which I've crept into since graduating from college. For the past several years, I've felt a need for directed study to replace my aimless "binges" of reading (lately replaced more and more frequently by even more aimless television watching). I've chosen writing, because of the encouragement of my grandmother, now a retired high school English teacher. She's long felt that I had talent for creative writing, but the harder she pushed the idea, the more stubbornly I resisted it.

Having outgrown that impulse to resist, I'm now expecting to find in the study of writing the self-discipline needed for the continual growth involved in developing a cultivated, "well-furnished" mind. This would be a major step toward achieving the greatest ambition of my life. . . the development of a disciplined character as the means to the higher good to an inner faith - the deep peace of the heart and mind, the Christian "peace of God, which passeth all understanding." (Philippians 4:7). The responsibility involved is well stated by Emerson, "Nothing can bring you peace but yourself; nothing can bring you peace but the triumph of principles."

More specifically, I hope to sharpen my awareness of the world and its peoples. I hope to discover and learn to express some of the truths of life. In particular, I'd like to help combat prejudices on some of its many levels. For me, writing is the most accessible and interesting of the arts or crafts which would satisfy a need for creative self-expression.

I have another incentive for studying writing. Upon completion of the Famous Writers School course, I plan to begin graduate studies at the nearby university. I'm sure learning to express myself clearly will be a major factor in the success of my efforts toward a master's degree. Conversely, my university studies should also add to my work as a writer.

A final, basic, although much less philosophical reason for my studying writing, is the chance of earning some money of my own. A career in writing seems to be one of the few part-time jobs which could enhance my major role in life, that of wife and mother. Writing, as our children grow older and home duties lessen, should increase from a part-time to a nearly full-time occupation.

Au Revoir

S he began to walk more rapidly down the street. Looking back quickly, only allowing herself one more glance, she saw the blue and gray of the bus envelope a tiny Citroën as Jack passed it on the Paris street.

"Funny," she mused to herself, "I'll probably never see them again." But as much as she knew she cared or might someday care; now she felt it didn't really matter. Time backward and time present seemed to disappear in importance. All her thoughts were directed to the future. Yet not the immediate future, that was too frightening, as time always is when it stands before an event. Nothing seemed to exist today.

Everything, even the blue sky and traffic noises belonged to tomorrow. Somehow, unbelievable as it still was, tomorrow she would arrive in New York City. The anticipation was maddening. "I've got to do something," she reasoned, "something meaningful; something I can care enough about to quit thinking like this." The plans she'd made to pass the lonely afternoon had faded. The Louvre and the Rodin museums were both closed on Tuesdays. She'd already walked to the Air Terminal twice to be sure she knew where she needed to go when the long awaited hour arrived. It would be foolish to go again. Perhaps one last walk down the Champs Elysees. No, she'd rather remember it as it was last night, brilliant and full of life, people in a gay hurry and people enthralled with the shops and the excitement, people who were walking slowly and taking long looks in the beautiful shop windows and at the exotic people passing by.

"Silly," she scolded her tardy thoughts, "what could be more fascinating than the bookstalls!" Every time she'd passed them she'd wanted to linger. Crossing the street to the river she scarcely noticed the absence of traffic. A moment later the roar of cars coming head-on at fifty miles an hour reminded her of that first evening in Paris when the fluxation of traffic amazed her. "Strange," she thought, "how little things like this become familiar so quickly." Yet other things couldn't be familiar. She wondered if they ever would be – the strange Gaelic reserve of the French one moment and the warm hospitality the next; the obvious distain some felt at the word American and the helpful little French lady who directed her to the UNESCO building. Brotherhood had seemed like such a simple thing when she had sat at home reading the papers. If only the barriers were merely language and skin color or national boundaries, but they weren't. They were individuals with strange ideas, unusual values, and concepts meaningless to her.

This wasn't helping her to quit thinking about the foreigners of her position. The bookstalls in this block were closed. The long green boxes were padlocked and looked as dull and ordinary as toolchests. The strange uneasy feeling tried to creep back into her mind unnoticed, but the tightening of her throat and the jumbled condition of her stomach gave fair warning. The questions panicked her again. What if she missed the plane? Where would she go? What would she do in a strange land thousands of miles from home and countries away from anyone she knew? When she looked up all the faces looked hostile and strange. The unintelligible language in her ears was maddening. It irritated her not to be even able to understand passing conversation or simple comments. Yesterday it was different; the conversation went unnoticed, hostile faces appeared friendly and smiling to the three American girls laughing and chatting eagerly about the things they were seeing. Now it was different. There was no one to point out the artist painting under the bridge; no one to confer with on which way was back to the hotel, and no one waiting at the hotel.

She thought about the bus speeding across the French countryside on the way to Le Havre. Jack, "The Flying Dutchman", would soon be taking his "car" as he called it, home to Holland after two months roaming about the continent. Surely the bus would seem strangely empty to him after it had served as a haven for hundreds of bundles of souvenirs and gifts which the girls had gathered all over Europe.

She glanced again at her watch, still hours more to go. The Seine below her looked busy but it too had lost its fascination. A woman on the flatboat tied up to the wall was listlessly hanging out a dingy wash. She looked bored but she didn't seem lonely. "She was lucky," the girl mused, "to be home, even if a flatboat was the only home she knew."

The crowd began to thicken and push in both directions. She edged out from the wall and moved into the flow of people toward the bookstalls. Each bookstall was an intriguing little library in itself. Antique books between dusty old maps and dog-eared modern pocket books soon claimed her attention. Occasionally ancient coins and knickknacks would catch her eyes but the books always reclaimed them. Stall after stall she moved on. She diverted her attention from the books only long enough to observe the book sellers, fully as intriguing as their merchandise. The little old woman stood off aways from her stall binding a new book with a plastic covering while she chatted with the proprietor of the next shop. The beautiful hunting prints she had in this cubbyhole were almost too much of a temptation. Counting her franks, she lacked a hundred of the price. A little horse book caught her eye, *Le Cheval dans l'Art et l'Histoire.* In hesitant French she inquired about the price. With a twinkle in her old eyes, the woman replied and then said kindly, "thirty American cents, s'il vous plait." She tucked the little book in the camera compartment of her purse.

"How could anyone be bored in Paris," she questioned herself. Yet she had to realize she was bored. "No," she argued, as she walked along, not bored but just too numb with anxiety to absorb her setting. Her mind flitted from one aspect of Paris to another but it still returned to dwell on the hour of her departure. "Someday," she smiled to herself, "I'll look back on this and it'll only be a passing instant when I glance at a travel poster of the Seine, or read the words, *Qui D'Crsay* in a book somewhere; but now it's so constant and real. Will this damn day never end?"

Her thoughts were broken as she noticed a few people standing in a circle. With typical American tourist agility she had her camera out by the time she reached the group. "I surely wish Linda were still here," she said half aloud, as she snapped a shot of the sidewalk artist at his work with bright yellow and orange chalk. She tried all week to get a picture like this. Maybe I can send her a print.

Her feet were beginning to drag even more than the time. She turned her watch over. She had put it face down in an effort to avoid glancing at it. "Still only four o'clock," she sighed. "Yet that's better than three or two or eleven this morning when the group left. They must be nearly to the boat by now." It was nice for once to have tired feet. They gave her something to think about. She crossed the street and turned left, back towards the hotel. She mused about who in the world she wanted to write another letter to. She had written seven this morning while the other girls were loading their things onto the bus. She had had her suitcases packed and ready since last night. The hotel's writing room had become boring and stuffy this morning but the chairs would be a welcome relief now.

Walking past the street to Saint Germain de Pres, a flood of memories from Sunday night returned. Down this street and then to the right into the Latin quarter – she had left a little bit of her love for music there. Someday she would return to the Abbaye, a little Paris night spot with barely room for thirty person, packed in with a hundred, and spend another evening listening to the ballads, recapturing the magic moments when artist, art and instrument became one. A particular ballad lingered in her thoughts, the last one they sang, *Time for man to go home.* Ironic, she thought; how she wished it were time for her to go home. Someday, she promised herself, she'd come back and walk down that very street and listen to Gordon and Lee sing, and whistle, and play, and the ballads and the people who sang them hundreds of years ago would come alive again for a moment. She knew she'd probably never come back but that was a hard thing to face, even with all her wishes set on returning home.

Somehow 6:30 came. She sat and watched the red second hand sweep down and overtake the two golden pointers, one obscuring the other. She rose deliberately and walked from the writing room. "A taxi, please," and the hall porter signaled for one of the uniformed men hovering near his desk. "The bags from room twelve," she said, as she pointed to the blue suitcase and the green canvas bag stuffed with packages. The taxi had swirled and made a u-turn on the broad Paris street and sat jiggling by the curb, its motor coughing spasmodically, "A la gare de Saint Lazare, s'il vous plait, monsieur." The driver smiled at the strange accent and edged the car away from the curb. "Darn it," she thought, "I meant to say, 'right down the street.' If he realized that I knew where it was he wouldn't drive around and run the meter up. Where did I read the warning? Fielding's, I guess. It's only a fifteen minute walk

10

though. He probably won't try it."

The voice droned over the air terminal mic, "Strange, it was a woman's voice," she mused. She had drawn out a pocketbook which she had saved all week just for this purpose. She began to read but this was an impossible task. She was no longer suffering from the lack of feeling which possessed her during the day. Suddenly the world was exciting again. She was flushed and aware of everything about her. The eagerness which she had tried so hard to ignore all day could no longer be restrained. It couldn't wear itself out now and turn to agony as eagerness does when time drags it through the minutes and the hours. She didn't have to worry about what she was going to do for the next few hours. Time had a master now. That master, her KLM flight schedule, would be just as merciless to time as time had been to her and her eagerness. People were milling about, some as aimlessly as she had all day, others, unconcerned, business-like; others, like herself, had a look of anticipation as sincere and as concentrated as that of a small boy hanging out the car window as he enters the State Fair gates.

The droning voice changed from the meaningless sounds of rapid French and German as it shouted to her, "KLM flight number 408 now boarding at gate ten." The announcer's English was good with barely a trace of accent. She got up hurriedly and was one of the first through the gate and onto the bus. As it pulled out of the terminal and towards the Seine, she watched the lights twinkling below on the boats. They crossed two of the big, sweeping, beautiful avenues that brought the magic of room and freedom of breath and movement to the city. She pressed her nose to the cool glass for a last look but surprisingly she felt no nostalgia. She had thought she would, for she had loved Paris.

After moments made hazy by excitement, she was on the large gray, red and white plane. It seemed now that the afternoon was far in the past, even farther away than this moment had seemed this morning. Now she didn't care about the afternoon; she never had. This was all that mattered, this and tomorrow. She would soon be on her way home - "Winging her way to New York." How exciting that sounds! She remembered indistinctly how maddening it had been. A month ago this moment was too far away to do any more than dream of it, and pretend, and talk; but this day, this whole day, when this moment was so close, it had never seemed farther away. But it had come; she was going home.

The Morning the Toad Sang

$\mathcal{E}$arly this summer as I was attacking a kitchen with dirty dishes climbing out of the sink and overflowing the counters, my little girl, Jessica, came running in.

"Come now, Mommy!"

Her brother, Pat, was pursuing a toad across the yard. She was sure he would get warts on his hands. I was sure the toad would get injured either by the boy or the two dogs who had joined in the chase.

I scooped up the toad. It soon settled down, cupped in my hands. We all lay down on the fresh grass; the children's faces were alive with eagerness to see the toad closeup. I put my

13

hands on the ground and then stroked the toad's rough back. He ducked his head, blinking his eyes, but remained calm. Gingerly, Jessica stroked the toad as I explained away the "wart story" she had heard from a child on the school bus.

Pat was eager to hold the toad in his over-zealous, four year old hands. He demanded "his toad" immediately. I watched fascinated, as the toad hopped casually from my hands across a few inches of grass and a tree root onto Pat's hand, pressed palm up in the grass. His face lit up with joy. He ventured cautiously to stroke the toad. He held his breath and began to caress it. He talked to it quietly.

Jessica and I watched from outside his world. Then, in the hush of the warm May morning, the toad began to chirp. "Listen, Mommy, he's singing us a song." Pat's round brown eyes shone. I was transfixed. The moments stood still until the toad hopped slowly from Pat's hand. Pat explained, "He's got to go home now." He hopped into a drain tile and out of sight. This was the first of many gentle meetings which highlighted our summer with "Pat's toad." I wish we could execute a "piaffe" and have this marvelous age of four just "trot in place." But, as it already rushes onto five, the memory of the morning the toad sang remains.

More Than One Way to Skin a Cat

His red ears flattened tightly against his head and she knew what would follow, but persistently she urged him again. "*Wham!*" His hoof bit into the cart and slivers of freshly varnished wood scattered in the dust. "Easy, Spook, no, quit," she repeated quietly.

"For God's sake quit talking to that damn horse and belt him one before he kills you!" Dave eased himself off the rail and went for a buggy whip.

"No," she replied, but not in the same quiet tone.

"Alright then, go ahead and get your teeth kicked in but you're ruinin' a good colt. If you'll just let me take him for a month, I'll have him runnin' on silk threads."

"We've been through this before. Let's forget it." She was standing beside the colt now, stroking the velvet spot on his nose.

"Okay," Dave tilted his hat back until the broad brim nearly touched the back of this neck. "I'll have you a little contest. The filly I'm working will drive circles around that spoiled brat of yours, backwards and forwards, before you even get him to down the lane. Give you a month."

"Nope, I'm in no hurry." She loosened the already drooping check rein and walked forward with the colt following as sleepy as a puppy.

"You teaching that animal to heel now? If you like to train dogs, why don't you get one and leave that colt to someone who can handle it?"

"Someone like you, I suppose," she didn't bother to look at him but fondled the colt's head as he poked it into her arms.

"That horse is goin' to bite your arm off one of these days."

"Probably," she said; she continued to stroke him.

"Has he ever bitten you?"

"No, I'll let you know when he does."

"Listen to me for a minute, would you? Next time he pulls that kicking stuff, I'll tell you what ya do. My filly did that just once. I put a 'running W' on her, ropes, you know; I'll rig one up for you. Pulls 'em right down on their knees."

"Thanks, but no thanks." She led the colt over to the rail and buckled the halter around his neck. She unbuckled the reins and throatlatch and eased the crown piece over his ears. He held the bit a minute and played with it. "Let go, would you, silly boy?" He released it suddenly and she reached to hang the bridle on the post.

"What did you do to the blinders on the bridle?" Dave picked it up and examined the nicks in the shiny new leather.

"Cut 'em off; he didn't much like them."

Dave muttered something about giving up as he threw the bridle down on the cart seat and went to his pickup.

"Aw, ca'mon little horse, just down the lane once. I'm not going to lead you again!" Spook pawed at the dust with short, quick strokes. She urged him on again. He switched his tail and caught her full in the face. "Ow, you ornery..." she brought the reins down hard on his rump. Both feet lashed out with splintering force. "Okay, sorry, boy. We're through for this day." She leaned out over his rump to stroke him gently with a clenched fist.

Dave's yellow pickup stopped as she led Spook back to the rail. "How's it going?" he called.

"Oh, so, so," she ducked her head down to pull at the rawhide that secured the tugs to the singletree. She looked up in a minute, giving the hot angry tears just enough time to disappear.

"Quittin' early today, aren't you? He givin' you trouble?"

"No, I'm givin' him trouble."

"Huh?"

"Never mind. Pull the cart into the barn, would you please?"

"Sure. Boy, that 'running W' really does the job. Has he kicked again with you?"

"Only when he feels like it."

"You're goin' to have to use it sooner or later. I'll bring my rope over as soon as the filly straightens out a bit. She's been jumping the traces once in a while but that rig brings her down every time."

"Uh, huh." Her thoughts wandered back to the anger welling within her. "Almost wish he'd kicked me, served me right, damn temper."

The sky was clear and the breeze nipped at her nose just enough to feel good. She could see Spook's red coat glisten in the sunlight. She called and he raised his head. The grass was still lush and he gave it a lingering tug as he began to walk toward her. "Today's the big day, Spook. It's nice and refreshing out and you're bound to feel like going all the way down the lane without stopping even once." He pointed his ears in answer as her hand drew some cattle cake and an apple out of her jacket. He jawed it slowly and nuzzled her for more. She turned and ran toward the barn. He followed closely and broke into a jolting canter as she raced down the little hill. He was breathing down her left shoulder and she shouted, "*Whoa*," as she swerved a bit at the gate. He slid to a stop and pushed his nose hard against her back. "Someday," she laughed between breathes, "one of us is going to goof and you're going to run me down. Hold up a minute while I put your halter on. There's real live cars running around on the other side of the fence, you know, and I wouldn't put it past you to try and play with one."

She led him up the dusty path to the barn. They both watched the buckskin and the black in the corral as they carried on a mock battle to relieve their boredom. The black planted a hoof a bit too solidly in the buckskin's flank. He squealed a protest and then walked over to see Spook. She let them converse a moment over the top rail before leading him up to the cart.

The Black Queen

Harold ran his hand gently over the smooth wood. He relished the silky feeling as his fingers moved from a mahogany square to a maple one and across into another dark square. The inlay work was perfect. The whole board was perfect, not a rough edge to be found. Harold followed a diagonal line of maple squares until he came to a lowly pawn, standing, feet firmly placed, on the blond wood. The woodcarver had endowed him with a head slightly off center. Harold picked him up and traced the rigid horizontal lines across his shoulders, then the edge of his coat and finally the stiff lines of his boot tops. He put the little fellow down and picked up the bishop directly behind him. The bishop had a look of power,

Harold thought, as he pushed this thumbnail into the design carved on the shield the bishop held staunchly in his left hand. His sword was poised for action. Harold remembered that action: Ander's bishop had swept out of the far corner of the board last game and picked off his knight, clean as a whistle. He'd needed that knight too. He placed the bishop back in his brown square and picked up the knight to his left. He loved the carving of his piece. The horse was rearing slightly, a nice stout horse with trappings carved into the dark wood. The knight sat him proudly, in full control of the beast. Harold picked some dust from the green velvet of the base of the knight's little wooden platform. He looked down on the carved turrets of the rook. It looked as stable and dependable as any castle could. "Long way from the king, thought." He turned to the old fellow and rubbed a speck of dust from his golden crown. "Poor old man, you're so all important but so power-less." Harold thought of where all the power was. He looked at her, standing there beside the king, but he didn't pick her up. The queen wore a gold crown which came nearly up to the king's nose as she stood beside him. Harold felt gently the delicately carved scepter and cross which the king held in his folded arms, and stared at the roughhewn sword, extending from her waist to the board, which the Queen grasped.

Harold thought of the first time he saw the set. He had walked past that import shop every day on his way to work.

He occasionally glanced in the window and on this particular morning, there it was, right in the center of the display. He stopped and searched for flaws in every figure. He'd never seen a chess set like that. The one Anderson had, the "Staunton design" was the nicest one he'd seen but it looked like a drab child's toy in comparison with the rich brown and delicate blonde of this beauty. He glanced at his watch, "Better hurry." He peered again into the display window. "Oh, well, what the hell; I've worked for old J.S. fifteen years. Guess I can be late once in a while."

He fingered first the smooth inlaid board and then the rough outline of the knight. The clerk leaned over his ear confidently. "Came in just this morning from Interlake, Switzerland – you know. It's expensive, of course, but every piece hand carved, exquisite." Harold managed to turn the little card around inconspicuously until he could finally read the price. "Well, yes, thank you. I'll think it over and stop back." Harold backed out the door and walked rapidly down the street.

The set had tantalized him for three weeks. One day he was panicked to find it had been removed from the window. He hurried into the shop and found a matronly woman examining the figures. "Yes, they would enjoy these little horses so. I'll be in again tomorrow." Harold hated to think of the set, his set, being subjected to that woman and her brats.

Harold felt proud and confident as he walked out of the import shop with the tightly wrapped box under his arm. "Just wait till Anderson sees this. Guess I'll even show it to old J.B."

Harold relished the looks of envy he got from the boys at the office. J.BN. was even impressed. "Quite a game, Taylor, quite a game. Funny though, I never thought of Effie as the type to play chess. Guess you never know." Harold smiled weakly as he carefully replaced the figures in the protective foam rubber lining of the box.

Harold glanced back at the board. "It was worth it," he muttered to himself and to the little wooden king, "every damn bit of it." Now he was convinced of this but for the first few weeks after he had brought the set home he couldn't enjoy looking at it this way. The brown and white always reminded him of the time payments of Effie's new fur stole. That damn mahogany queen with the folds carved so delicately in her long dress was the hardest one to enjoy looking at, even now, that the payments were half through.

Harold glanced at his watch. He didn't have much more time to admire his treasure. Effie'd be home from bridge club by five. "Good God!" He'd forgotten to put the potatoes on. He jumped from the chair and hurried into the kitchen. In a few minutes he returned and settled carefully into the stiff antique provincial chair. He'd been sitting right in this spot when he'd beaten Anderson. "What a game!" He couldn't remember a more exciting moment in his life than when he'd taken Anderson's black bishop with his white queen, and then Anderson had confidently taken his white queen only to discover as Harold delivered the final blow with his white knight, that Anderson's black king was unable to move out of check because he was hemmed in by his own black rook and bishop. "What a game!" But that was nearly a month ago. Effie's Lady's Aid society only met once a month during the evening.

Harold carefully arranged the little wooden figures into the positions of the last move of the pattern which he had been carefully working out for two weeks. He was on the eighteenth move now. This month he was playing with white to win, and he'd set up his cream colored army into good positions. This was, as well as he could remember from the article, the approximate way it had been when Aaron Nimzovich (White) had played A. Hakansson in the match at Kristianbad in 1922. That must have been some game. Harold hadn't been able to put the magazine down until he'd read the article four times word for word. He remembered how upset he'd been, one day carrying the garbage out, to discover that the entire end of the game had been soaked up by coffee grounds. He had rescued a sheet or two but Effie had burned them. "The filthy things," she had said, "you've gone crazy; the very idea of keeping garbage soaked papers in my house." Harold shook his head as he thought of it again, but at least he remembered enough to work on the moves.

"Let's see," he muttered, "where was I? Oh, yes." He moved the last piece into its former place. "White was preparing to attack the queen and king. White had played pawn takes queen's pawn, and this capture had opened the queen's bishop's file. Black's queen and king stood naked and exposed on an open file. Black hastily moved his king to queen one to get out of the line of attack, and White has played rook to queen bishop one." Harold took a second to contrast the power of this rook, sweeping the entire file with its deadly fire, with the tangled confusion in Black's enemy camp. "Let's see now, Black's attacked queen makes her one and only playable move to knight three." Harold checked over Black's position again. Some pieces were completely blocked and couldn't move at all. Others could only make meaningless and ineffective moves.

Harold moved his pawn to rook five and now his infantry comes to grips with Black's most valuable piece. The queen's rook's pawn stabbed at the Black queen and ordered her Royal Highness to move. Harold surveyed the board. "But where could she go?" Every square but one was commanded by the forces of his army. Harold smiled again as the queen had to make an ignominious retreat for her life. He moved her to the only available square, rook two, and then played his pawn to knight six. Again his pawn infantry had advanced. Another bayonet thrust, this time by the queen's knight's pawn, ordered the Black queen to again retreat. Harold unconsciously rubbed his hand along the edge of the board. "Was a queen ever treated so disrespectfully?" Harold had left only one place for the queen to go. He moved her carefully and placed her in rook one, leaving her to sulk in the corner. He sat back and surveyed her. Her position was almost incredible. Unable to move, completely hemmed in, it would have taken a major operation to extricate her. He moved his knight carefully into position; he was relishing each L-shaped move.

Harold started as the door slammed and Effie called from the kitchen, "Harold, get in here and put these groceries away. I'd certainly have thought a grown man could have remembered these little things when he shopped, but at any rate, I took time out from Bridge club to pick them up," her voice trailed off as she shut the bathroom door.

"Yes, Effie-love, right away."

Harold moved his rook over to guard the file toward which his knight was moving. Black had no useful moves left, so quite fairly, he moved a black pawn meaninglessly. He looked again at the queen hovering, helpless, in her little corner. He picked up the knight, caressing its square carving and moved it in position for the final kill. He moved another black pawn aimlessly.

"Harold, for heaven's sake, quit playing with your little

toys. The milk's getting warm."

Harold swept the knight into the corner and watched the trapped queen tumble to the floor. He smiled. "Yes, dear, coming right away."

Scarlet Ribbons

*C*arl edged the Dutch door of the barn open a little further. The wedge of yellow light struck first on the dirt tracked in from the corral, then it illuminated the stalks of broomcorn scattered on the floor; it glinted off the heavy pan which the cats drank milk from, and barely reached between the flat, rough boards which marked the beginning of the first stall. Next to it, in the corner, another light dimly reached out almost to the narrowed point where the wedge of light from the door finished.

Carl squinted into the shadows of the second stall. Nothing moved. It looked empty but he knew it was not. Soon it would be, he thought. The sooner the better; if only this whole damn mess were over. It bothered him. Carl could feel it working on him. It was a strange experience for him. He had seen death before; it had never really upset him, but this did, and he cursed himself silently for the weakness.

He pushed the door open silently. The wedge of light grew but it still did not reach the shadows which the little bulb over the stall cast. He walked carefully over the broomcorn. His boots still made noise wherever he placed them. He swore softly at a white hen which clucked as she pulled her beak from under her wing. "God-damned chicken," he said, "I didn't even touch you."

Carl looked into the stall. He wanted to look away and not look back but he forced his eyes to focus on the little mound in the center of the stall. Melinda's blond braids were draped down into the filly's mane and appeared to be tangled in the sorrel horse hair. Carl slipped the chain loop from the nail and walked into the stall. He didn't bother to latch the gate behind him. He stooped over his sleeping daughter. The six-foot bulk of his body cast another shadow under the dim bulb. He bent down slowly and began to lift the slender frame of the child. She stirred. "The little brat..." He gently replaced her and attempted to untangle the blond strands from the red horse hair with which they were braided. Melinda moved again to draw the little horse closer to her. Carl took his hands away but still squatted on the cane. He felt furry skin between the horses forelegs. It seemed as though the body warmth had already begun to leave. "God, how I hate it, but I've still got to do it." Carl's face was tense and strained. He kept unbraiding as Melinda stirred again. He looked into her face and watched as she opened her eyes slowly.

"Hi Daddy, did you come to check on Scarlet? We're taking good care of her,"

"Time for bed, my little lady." Carl tried to keep his voice casual but he failed. He glanced at his watch; 2 a.m. "In fact it's way past time." His hands rapidly untwisted the hair.

"Oh, you go ahead," Melinda yawned widely. "I want to stay so Scarlet won't be afraid when she wakes up."

"Damn it." He wanted to say; "You little fool the damn horse is dad. It's not asleep," but he couldn't. He couldn't even order her to get up and come in the house. He couldn't say a word.

He wished she'd cry. She hadn't cried at all. At first he dreaded it. He knew the way her tears tore at him, just a little no matter how hard he fought it. But even that would be better than her trust. Thank God, it wasn't faith in him. He wouldn't have to be the one who had failed her. He had told her quite simply that he had done all he could and it wasn't enough. Melinda had accepted it in a matter-of-fact way as though she had never really thought that saving her pony's life was Carl's responsibility. He'd tried and that was all she'd asked of him.

He had even called Dr. Hardin, the best vet in the three county area, but after Carl had described the colt's condition to him, Dr. Hardin told Carl he hated to charge him for an 80 mile call just to look at a dead pony; he knew also that the doc was thinking that he couldn't afford any more unpaid bills for a half-breed horse, but at least he didn't say it.

Melinda had pillowed her head on the colt's neck and she blinked her eyes in an effort to stay awake.

"Sweetheart," Carl's voice was soft, "you've got to come to bed now. Scarlet's not going to need you anymore."

"Oh, I know." Melinda's blue eyes were clouded with sleep, "God's perfectly able to take care of her but I'm sure she'd like to have me here too when she wakes up."

Carl hated his thoughts as he imagined Melinda waking in the morning to find her pony cold and stiff in her arms. His stomach knotted painfully as he thought of his little child hugging the dead animal.

Carl grabbed Melinda's shoulders and shook her. "You've got to be sensible. Scarlet's dead. Can't you realize that?"

Melinda looked up. Her face seemed at first amazed and then her eyes dismissed Carl's face with a second look.

Carl waited for her tears to finally come, but they didn't She said simply, "Scarlet's sleeping. God won't let her die."

Carl stood up. The palm of his hand stung as he hit it with the big knuckles of his other hand. Melinda had laid her head back on the sorrel hair and closed her eyes.

The Dutch door creaked as he latched it behind him. Carl tapped the tobacco quickly into the thin white paper. He rolled it carefully and licked the edge before pressing it gently down. He fumbled in his Levi's for a match and struck it against the wooden post.

The moon was bright and Carl traced the outline of the mesa to the west. He could even make out the individual trees along the ridge. The cool morning air made him shiver. He wished he'd brought a jacket but he knew it wouldn't be worth going back to the house for it. He couldn't face Elizabeth. He thought of her. She was probably still sitting in the rocker opposite the kitchen door. She'd be jerking her head abruptly, trying to keep awake. She always sat there when he went over his records in the evening. She would be knitting, or reading, or brushing her long yellow hair, but she would always be there until he was ready to go to bed.

Damn! Elizabeth had started this business. Why couldn't she come out here and finish it? She was the one who said grace at every meal, and insisted on Melinda's bedtime prayers, and now Bible reading. Every night that damn Bible reading. She'd never pushed Carl. She always invited him to read with them but she'd never pushed him. He always sat with his back to them reading the paper and listening to Melinda's voice alternate with her mother's on every other verse.

Carl ground his half-smoked cigar into the dirt with the rounded heel of his boot. It was all her fault. He hadn't even wanted to get the fool animal. He ground the cigarette harder as he admitted to himself that if Elizabeth hadn't consented first that he would have. Melinda had fallen in love with the little filly and neither had seriously considered refusing her prayers. She had never asked them for it. She had merely said that God was giving her Magill's new filly and that she hoped it would be all right with them. Elizabeth was thrilled when Melinda had said this one morning at breakfast but Carl had laughed and said, "Oh, and is God going to feed it, too?" But he had only been kidding and Melinda laughed although Elizabeth didn't.

Carl kicked his foot slowly against the corral post. This was where he had first snubbed the little weanling filly. But she hadn't really even needed a halter rope. She followed Melinda like a puppy. He thought of that first day when he gathered the colt up in his arms and lifted it down from the pickup bed.

At first Melinda just stared at the wobbling colt in front of her. "Daddy," she said. "Daddy," she repeated without taking her eyes off the little red animal, "isn't she the beautifulest creature in the world?"

"Not bad," Carol answered, "for fifteen dollars. Magill's mare has good colts." He turned to Elizabeth. "He was so mad when he found that little Shetland stud of Marshall's in with that registered Quarter mare of his, he was ready to shoot him both instead of just that feisty little pony. He still gets mad when he talks about it... wouldn't even let the little filly suck his mare another day when he found out I'd give him fifteen for it." Carl glanced back toward the filly and Melinda. The little horse was nuzzling and bumping her with its nose. "You've got your work cut out for you, young lady. That little animal is going to have quite an appetite. Maybe if you ask your Mom, real polite-like, she'll show you how to rig up those bottles I gave you yesterday."

Melinda spent hours every day brushing and fussing with the little colt. A week went by before she named it. Carl walked into the corral and stopped short as Melinda and the colt ran into him and knocked him back a step. "Whoa," he shouted, as he grabbed Melinda and tossed her high above his head. She came back into his arms giggling.

"Guess what?" she said loudly. Her impish little nose wiggled as she laughed.

"What?" said Carl with mock anticipation.

"We've named her, mama and I. Guess what we call her." Melinda's voice was demanding as she pointed at the little pony.

Carl laughed at the filly's comical face. Her short forelock had been braided into three braids and tied with bright red ribbons. Huge red bows clashed with the sorrel hairs sticking straight up in her mane.

He tried to keep his face straight as he mused. "Hmmm, let's see now. Oh, I bet I know."

"What?" Melinda shouted.

"Blueboy."

Melinda pouted for a second. "Oh, daddy, of course note; Scarlet's a girl."

"Oh," said Carl, "I see. Well, Scarlet's a pretty name."

"But that's not all," Melinda insisted, "it's Scarlet Ribbons Random..."

"Of the Carl, Elizabeth, and Melinda Random ranch," Carl finished.

"How'd you know, Daddy?" Melinda was wide-eyed for only a moment.

"Oh," Carl said, hoisting Melinda up on his shoulders, "a little bird told me on her way past the garage to fix the lunch we're going to be late for if we don't hurry."

A bull growled softly off to Carl's left, beyond the cotton-woods. Carl peered into the moonlit sage but couldn't distinguish the shape of an animal. "One of the three year olds must have jumped the cattle guard again. Have to check on it when it's light." Carl mused for a moment or two on what he needed to accomplish today, where he needed to go, what cows he'd have to check on, whether he'd have time to fix the windmill up north; no, better look after the lame heifer first; to pursue each idea, but it persistently returned to Melissa and the filly.

Carol crossed the corral slowly and opened the Dutch door with fumbling movements. He started towards the stall when the sound of Melissa's voice stopped him. Even in the early morning silence, he had to listen closely to make out any words. He could see her bending over the filly. Her head was bent until her upturned nose rested lightly on the tips of her clasped fingers. "Please dear God, help all the animals and children all over the world, and especially Becky, and Susie, and Scotty, and please may Scarlet wake up soon so Daddy won't have to worry anymore." Melissa's lips were still moving but Carl couldn't make out anymore words. He watched until she sank back into the bedding beside the little horse.

"Damn it," Carl muttered. "Damn it all anyhow," as he shut the stable door softly. "Why don't I just do something?" Carl turned sharply. "There's no reason," he argued with himself. "Why I can't just walk in there and carry her up to the house. It'll be better for her. She's got to face it." Carl stopped at the door without opening it. He stood there, staring at the dim shape of the rawhide latch. He looked over his shoulder, across the long end of the corral, to the moon. He knew it was beautiful, but it didn't seem beautiful to him now.

Carl thought of Melinda. He thought of the time he'd

grabbed her just as her baby hand had reached towards a rattler coiled under the kitchen steps. God, that'd scare him; he'd chopped the snake's head off with the hoe before he even stopped to think. He remembered when he'd opened the corral gate and started to drive the bulls in, only to discover Melinda sitting in the dust playing with her puppy. One of the old range bulls had started after the pup but Carl had gotten Melinda up behind the saddle before the bull reached them. "Why don't I do something about this?" Carl shook his head slowly. He looked up. There were clouds over the moon now. "If only it were a man trying to break her heart, I could fight him. I could explain it to her. But I can't fight...." Carl's head jerked up as he heard the kitchen door being shut. It sounded a million miles away but it startled him into action.

He grasped the latch and opened the stable door quickly. He walked deliberately toward the stall. He braced himself mentally for the sight. The filly would be getting stiff by now. He might have to pull Melinda away from the cold little form if she woke up.

Carl stopped suddenly. He stared through the open stall door. His first impulse was to hurry into the stall but he merely stood and stared.

Scarlet's ears moved attentively as she paused in her rhythmic licking to look at Carl. Carl continued staring at her. She was resting lightly on her side and stomach. She had one foreleg tucked under her and the other extended straight out across Melinda's tightly curled little legs. Melinda had one arm around the filly's neck and had pillowed her blond head in the thick red hair of Scarlet's shoulder. She was sleeping soundly and only stirred a little as Scarlet resumed her rough bathing of Melinda's check and her own matted red hair.

Carl was nearly running when he met Elizabeth at the corner of the corral. She had thrown his old mackinaw over her shoulders and her long blond hair was unbraided. She didn't look at his face when she asked where Melinda was. Before Carol could answer, Elizabeth blurted, "So help me if you've left her with that dead colt...." She shut her mouth in the middle of the sentence. She opened it again, "I'm sorry, Carl; it's rough enough, isn't it?" Carl put his arm around her quaking shoulders and led her gently to the open top of the Dutch door.

Elizabeth had cried all the way back to the house. She sobbed softly though and Melinda never woke up until her Daddy's hands released her onto her bed. She smiled sleepily as she cuddled under the covers her mother was tucking in.

Elizabeth's tears had disappeared and her eyes were shining when she returned from upstairs. Carl was sitting with his back to the stairs. He was warming his hands around a steaming cup of coffee, and he stared out the window at the faint flow of pink in the eastern sky. Orange tinges were beginning to illuminate the trees. It was beautiful.

Elizabeth kissed his forehead gently without stopping on her way to the icebox. "Eggs sunnyside up?" she asked between snatches of a tune she was humming.

"Yeah," Carl took his eyes from the window and turned to look at his wife. Her hair was pulled back into neat braids now and her housecoat swished about her slim figure. "What's that you're singing?"

"Oh, I don't know," Elizabeth's hands deftly cracked two eggs into the pan, "can't remember the words, tune just came to me."

Carl turned back toward the window. The sun was nearly up now. Carl remembered the words, but only snatches of them. "I saw my child at prayer... if I live to be a hundred, I'll never know from where came those scarlet ribbons, scarlet ribbons, for her hair."

I'm Pooh

I lay on the rug and watched the Mrs. dust the venetian blinds. I wished she'd quit it. She'd be sure to scare all the birds away before it was time for my daily outing on the porch. Guess I'll just have to make the sacrifice, I sighed. Hate to bother her with my problems when she's so upset with her own.

Perhaps I'd better introduce myself before I go much further. My name's "Pooh." I thought at first that I had been named after A.A. Milne's immortal character, "Winnie the Pooh" but one day last month when I was taking a sunbath in the library I came across one of the Boss' books lying open on the desk. I thought I recognized the word at the top of the page and sure enough it was the same as the one painted over my bed, "Pulicidae." Probably a famous general or warrior, I figured. The Boss had told the Mrs. right after I came to live with them that I had to have a Latin name since my mother was obviously a Roman. I read a little farther, and, well, it's really not worth talking about; but I've never quite forgiven them. It seems incredible they could have so warped a sense of humor as to name a self-respecting cat after the family name for fleas.

The morning had gone pretty well except for a few minor calamities, the worst of which occurred when the Mrs. let the hound in from next door. I put him in his place right off when he headed toward my food bowl but it was exhausting to go from rug to rug to keep him from finding a place to lie down. Sometimes I wonder just how much nerve these people have, letting that cur into my house.

I doubt if you can appreciate my situation but I actually have a tough full-time job here. This is the first family I've ever had to watch after and it's getting to be a real problem. To complicate matters I'm the first overseer they've ever employed so it's a mess trying to break them in. They've only been married a few months and aren't even used to being bossed by each other yet so my authoritarian rule gets 'em down once in a while. It's the only way to handle humans thought. Course, I've got to be subtle once in a while, let 'em think they're pretty important, especially around mealtime on Fridays, but generally I just go ahead and take matters in my own paws.

Well, this particular day I started to tell you about, I was being a vulture. It gets kind of boring around here, you know, so a cat's got to use his imagination to keep busy. Sometimes I'm a lynx, or a tiger, but this day I was being a vulture. I was sitting on top of the refrigerator staring down at the Mrs. as she prepared lunch. I was giving her the steady stare I always use when I'm waiting for a victim to die, and it was kinda getting through to her. She'd glance at me uneasily once in a while and almost cut her hand slicing a tomato.

"Honey," she exclaimed as the Boss walked in the door, "there's something wrong with Pooh. He's been staring at me for half an hour." As the Boss walked over to the refrigerator, I decided I'd rather be a tiger so when he reached up to pet me I grabbed his hand in my claws and started to bite. "Oh, so you want to play, you little lion," he began. I nearly corrected him and said "tiger" but decided it wasn't worth it since he was now ruffling my fur and I had to defend myself. As the Boss extricated his hand from my mouth he said, "He's all right, he just wants to play. Why don't you throw his mouse for him?"

Oh no, I thought, if they drag out that silly mouse again... they've got this stupid stuffed mouse that smells awful, not at all like a nice rat that's been dead a few days, and they persist in throwing it across the floor. I try to humor 'em and run after it but it's certainly a ridiculous way to spend an afternoon. Someday when I'm bigger and they let me outside, I'm going to get a real mouse and bring it to the Mrs. I'll bet she'll really throw that one across the floor.

I jumped down from the refrigerator and sat on the counter. I knew I had to be on my toes for this meal so I wanted to be right down where I could work. The Boss (I only call him that out of courtesy; actually they're even beginning to understand the situation. Just the other day the Mrs. said, "You'd think that cat owned the place, the way he's taken over our bed." My favorite spot happens to be right in the middle of it. The mattress fits my back just right there.) Well, anyway as I was saying, the Boss was in a bad mood at breakfast so I needed to be prepared for a busy meal. I tried to warn the Mrs. this morning to avoid the week's controversial subject since I'd seen the Boss drop his new razorblade in the spring, and I'd heard what he'd said. I always hang around in there in the mornings to watch the whirlpool. It's sure fascinating.

Before I even got settled by the stove, she began. "We got another letter from my folks, honey. Would you like me to read it to you?"

"Huh?" the Boss looked up from his soup. He had been steadily contemplating a gray and yellow hair which looked rather conspicuous as it floated leisurely in and out amount the bits of chicken and noodle. I've always thought the texture of my fur was quite exquisite but I never realized the Boss was so impressed with it. I had to crane my neck to watch him gently remove it with his spoon and reverently wipe it on his napkin. "Oh, no; no, haven't got time now," he frowned as he answered, evidently due to the interruption of his contemplation on the remarkable symmetry of the coloring on my cat hair.

The Mrs. continued with a few choice excerpts from the letter all to the effect that it had been a long time since they'd seen them. "Wouldn't it be wonderful," she said, "if we could take your two weeks' vacation next month to go back to see them?"

"You mean take my two weeks fishing trip to drive three days to go back to that muddy lake in Indiana when we've got the finest trout streams in the nation only thirty miles from us? I thought you'd agreed to drop this subject this morning."

"Well, that's not fair. That was before I got this letter. Do you realize we haven't been back since we were married."

"Do you realize we've only been married seven months?"

"But Sweetheart..."

Oh, oh, I thought. I'd best get busy. I walked quietly out of the kitchen and then dashed under the sofa. Sure enough, my plaintive yowls brought them immediately. They both stooped down to peer under the sofa and immediately burst out into laughter. I was striving to look as ridiculous as possible and evidently I attained my goal. I was lying on my back with all four feet hooked into the under covering of the sofa.

The Boss gently removed my claws from the matting and hauled me out onto the rug. They both sat there and laughed. One of the most self-sacrificing achievements in the world for a cat is to allow himself to be laughed at. Every sound hurt. Fortunately the boss reconciled me when he said, "Just showing off your pheasant belly weren't you, Pooh?" I purred a condescending answer. Perhaps you'll think I'm bragging but I actually am known as the pleasantest bellied cat in the State. My stunning combination of yellow and gray stripes seems to resemble very closely the stomach of a pheasant, or at least so my Boss says. I've never seen a pheasant but I'm sure it must be very noble and intelligent beast. Someday I'm going to find out what it is exactly as soon as they leave the dictionary open to "ph-". Once it was open to "po-" but I couldn't find anything about me. Guess it must be a pretty old edition.

At any rate my mission was accomplished and the Boss went back to work before another word of argument got started. The afternoon was rather uneventful. I tried to help the Mrs. type a letter to her folks. I always do my best to keep those little metal things from marring her pretty letter paper. Sure hurts when they hit my nose, though. Fortunately after a few minutes she thinks it's too tough a job for me and puts me out on the porch to take over the sparrow patrol.

She let me in in time to supervise the cooking of dinner. I okayed the porkchops and checked out a little muffin batter she had just mixed. I suddenly noticed that she had gone ahead and put some clothes in the drying machine (this is quite similar to the washing machine except that it's much nicer in that it has a little window and no water). I've always been in complete charge of this operation and it rather upset me that she hadn't waited. Carefully watching the clothes tumble by took up my time for the fifteen minutes before the Boss got back from work. This is quite a trying responsibility and I was much too dizzy to finish my piece of porkchop fat before dinner so I carried it into the bedroom for safekeeping. I've sure got to watch these people. Every once in awhile they take my food back again. I haven't figured out why they're so greedy but they seem especially angry when I carry fish in on the new sofa.

Dinner started off pretty well but it took a turn for the worse when the doorbell rang and the Boss had to walk past the maps of Colorado, Kansas, Missouri, Illinois and Indiana, which were spread out on the sofa. By the time he got back through Indiana and stumbled over all 50 States in the American Road Atlas which I had pushed on the floor, he was furious. "I thought we'd ended this thing again," he shouted, "what kind of mental persecution are you starting?"

The Mrs. immediately burst into tears but it didn't work this time. Guess she'd forgotten that Mr. Davis said that only works for about the first two months and they'd been married over seven. I knew I had to do something quickly but I wasn't sure what. Since this was such an emergency, I decided to risk my pride, and a little pain so I dashed into the living room and over to the chess set on the coffee table. Slowly and deliberately I raised my paw and wacked the end chessman. It was quite round so it made a nice long rolling sound on the hardwood floor until it bumped softly into a shag rug. The sound of one of his hand-carved chessmen hitting the floor was too much for the Boss. He was in the room before I could skuttle under the sofa. He had me cornered by the bookcase but I shot through his legs and made it into the bedroom and under the bed to safety. If only they'd realize what I go through for them!

Even with such formidable risks it was worth it since the rest of the meal was finished in comparative peace. I could hear the Boss muttering, "Can't figure out what gets into that damn cat, he hasn't touched that chess set for a couple of months." Unfortunately this was the lull before the storm. After dinner Mrs. Davis called and the Boss answered the phone. As she gushed out, "Oh, Mr. Craig, I'll bet you're just thrilled about your trip to Indiana." I laid my ears back and crawled under the radiator. The Boss barely managed to hand the phone to the Mrs. and retreated to his den. The minute the

47

Mrs. hung up the phone he was out again. "Okay, now," he said softly, "let's try to work this out like calm, reasonable people. We'll just sit down and you can present your views first and then I'll state mine, and we can discuss them quite civilly and rationally." It wasn't five minutes before they were shouting again. I crawled out from under the radiator resignedly and headed for the living room. I wasn't about to try the chess set again. The Boss was so furious he'd probably put me down the basement for a week, and if I broke another of the Mrs.'s figurines, she'd be sure to put me back on milk rations since she knows how I love my cream. I reasoned that these alternatives were certainly above and beyond the call of duty.

Suddenly I hit upon the perfect solution. As soon as they heard the racket I was making they both came into the room. The Boss burst out laughing then he saw me clawing my way through Kansas and biting at Missouri with a little bit of the Colorado map stuck to my tail. Even the Mrs. had to smile as I ferociously leaped into the middle of Illinois. "Well, that settles it, he said with a smile," if the owner of this corporation says no, we certainly can't fight it."

"No, I guess not," she said, "I can't fight both of you. Besides, it might be even more fun to go back next Christmas."

"Unless they open a winter trout season," the Boss smiled as he put his arms around her.

I crawled out of Illinois but decided to stick my nose back

into Indiana. I do wish they wouldn't carry on with these displays of affection in front of me. After all it's highly embarrassing for a bachelor cat in my position.

For Trefa

O cat, wise cat, cat of my heart
Gone now.
I miss you.
Gone from fuzzy youth
Gone from supple prime
Released now from failing old age.
I miss your special mouse call,
Summoning me to admire your catch.
I miss your incredible spring from floor
    to great height.
I miss your twitching tail,
    your eloquent expressions of disdain.
I miss your affectionate rubs and purrs.
I miss you, Witch, Bit of the Wild,
    Come to share your mystery with us,
    Gone to great mysteries.

Farewell to Starboy

Mane tossing in the sun,
Power, gentleness,
Rhythm and cadence,
Great hairy shoulder to cry on,
Warm soft breath of nuzzling.

Pointed ears flickering forward, alternating,
One ear back, listening above the rushing wind.
All now still, lying motionless in the straw,
Incredible spark and flame of life gone.

Goodbye – Goodbye, Beloved one –
God be with you until we meet again –
To gallop down the frosty ridges of the nigh,
To leap off and fly with Pegasus to the Moon.

Starboy 1956-1970
May 22, 1987
Milliron Farm, Athens, Ohio

Gray Galloper

The day was clear with white clouds like big dips of ice cream on a blue dish. It was warm, almost muggy, and I knew that by this afternoon Ohio showers would send me scurrying for home.

That doesn't matter now, nothing does. It was a free day, the wind was free in the trees, the sun was free to ripple, and best of all I was free to run, run – out the kitchen door, across the rough terrace stones, bounding in one, two, three, four, and nearly five jumps across the asphalt driveway and into the alley.

Down the alley past Hattman's, *whoops*, there's Linda

and Stevie. Mustn't let them see me. Behind Rann's hedge, sneak along it, and across to the twisted apple tree. Got to stop and check on the robins. Peering up into the branches with lots of green leaves, brown bark and twigs, ah, there they are, the white string always gives away the little home. Wonder how long it'll be before the pipes will fall. Still can't say that word Gary told me... Ca... Catawba.

Black lightening tossed his head, rolled his eyes, and snorted; prancing a little he edged out from the shade of the trees. With mincing steps, the white stagecoach road was crossed; he hesitated a moment, looking up and downstream before plunging into the black murky waters of the river, scrambling up the other bank, he started across another narrow path.

Oh, oh, that car coming looks like ours, clearing the rest of the sidewalk in a leap, I ducked into Rondell's shrubs. Coast is clear, down the alley, across Maple; gosh, is this the street to the park or is it the next one. Guess I'll go across; that house surely doesn't look familiar, or that garage, or this white fence, maybe I should go back; maybe Mom misses me already. No, I won't.

It's not far now, it can't be. Maybe that big man would know, but maybe he'd ask me who I am. Maybe I shouldn't have come down the alley. Sure, a lot of junk here by the garages. Gee, that boat's pretty, wonder if they'd mind if I'd climb on it for just a little while. Sure, would be fun to haul on that wooden wheel like in the movies. All we'd need would be a stepladder beside it for a crow's nest and we could play pirate. Bobbie, Huey, and Sallie would think this was keen, but then our mom's 'll never let us come way over here.

Here kitty, kitty. Pooh, go ahead and run anyhow, 'fore I throw a stone at you. Wonder what that glinting is, guess I'd best check it out. It's... it's a horse! Oh, he's beautiful. His neck arches just like the Black's, pretty pointed ears, his chest is broad and cool, trim legs. His little hoofs fit in my hands. They curl back nearly to his tummy. His tail's broken a little and his back hoof is chipped but he's beautiful. His back's sure warm, must be the sun. Hope he doesn't mind it. Wonder if he lived on a merry-go-round like the one in the park. He must have been a pretty spirited fellow. He still looks like he'd love to run. We could go like the wind, across the arroyos on the prairie, down the hill to the woods. Gee, but Bobbie 'd think he was keen, but I wouldn't let him ride him, not for a while at least. It'd sure be fun to fix up a little stall in the garage. I could use boxes and maybe Daddy 'd get me some straw for him. I'd sure like to sit on him, but maybe then they'd come out of the house and be mad and wouldn't give him to me. Wonder who owns him, surely nobody loves him. He's so scratched and rusty, poor thing. I bet Garry 'd let me use his brushes and paint. The mane and tail would be pretty dark gray, with a red bridle and saddle, and his name and mine on the saddle blanket. Guess his eyes are still pretty brown. I don't like his red nostrils though. Wonder if Gary could fix it. This hole in his mouth must be for a rein. Guess I could use the braid I made for Sport. He doesn't like it anyhow. Always lays down and chews on it. Maybe I'll make a new one for – what will I call him? Misty, no, he's too ornery; ought to be a gray name, though, Gray Galloper. How'd you like to be named that? Wonder what the raised metal on his chest is for. Where's it go? From the saddle down across his chest, through his front legs and back to the girth.

Gee, he's pretty and just the right size. Wonder if I could lift him; oh, pooh, he's way too heavy to carry, but Daddy could take him real easy and put him in the car. It' might be time for him to be home. I'll have to hurry.

Bye, Gray Galloper, don't leave, I'll be back for you, and you'll love your new home, and we'll gallop and gallop, and I'll pet you and brush you, and feed you. We'll have a swell time. I'll be back. Gee he looks even prettier from a distance. I'm glad that flouncy old bush hides him, nobody else 'd even know he's there. Wonder if I can run all the way home.

Cruising Down the River

The leaf drifted lazily below her. She dipped her paddle in carefully and watched it swirl and disappear with the stroke. She stroked again and again, but the bank seemed the same, the water seemed the same, Ann's back, moving rhythmically with each stroke, seemed the same as it had been hours ago.

"Let's switch, okay?" she said, as she automatically swung her paddle in an arc over the middle thwart; the water droplets glistened as they fell in a semi-circle on the canvas pack. Ann muttered an answer, "May as well." She shifted her paddle in the same moment. The steady paddling continued. The muddy banks, steeply cut away, passed by more slowly now. This morning the rolling green meadows and tree lined shores had hurried by and the river paid them no heed. But here, the river had been cruel to the banks, and had mercilessly cut them into slippery sheets of mud.

"I wish we could stop," Ann's voice was matter of fact, as it interrupted the gentle sounds of the waves and the occasional thump of a paddle against the canoe.

"Well," Jo replied with irritation, "have you seen any place for the last hour?"

"No, course not, but I just thought maybe you were tired too but I guess it doesn't matter," Ann's voice trailed off as she lost interest in the idea.

"There's an island ahead. See it?" Jo peered around the bend and caught a glimpse of the large clump of trees and bushes in the middle of the river.

"Looks like a big one," she answered enthusiastically, "there's bound to be a spot there." The water began to rush as it split on the point of the island. The largest amount ambled off to the left and a smaller dashed into the opposite bank and careened on around the island.

"Where are you heading?" Ann called back anxiously as the canoe was caught up in the excitement of the current.

"On the left bank, can you see a place?"

"No, it's still a muddy mess, but let's head around the left side; it looks like the main branch."

"Suits me. That other side looks a bit tricky," Jo answered

as she dug her paddle into a backstroke and the bow swung gracefully into the left channel. The current was swifter than she had expected for such a broad channel. "Hey, Ann, did you notice how swift this current is?"

"No, not 'specially," she replied without much interest; her attention was centered on the island's shore.

"Don't' strain your eyes, Ann; these campsites don't look too choice."

"I can't figure it out," her disillusioned answer was barely audible over the slapping waves.

"I think it has," Jo replied, "look at all the junk in the branches." She pointed to the dead leaves and grass, matted and clinging to stripped branches.

"Good heavens," Ann, exclaimed, "some of that stuff is six feet off the ground."

"Yeah," Jo replied, "and it must have stayed that way awhile, look at the waterline." The gray filmy line stretched regularly from bush to bush. Ann's eyes followed it for a moment and then she sighed, "This is hopeless; the whole place is just mud and gook."

The island curved ahead and Jo swung the canoe out to clear a small mud covered log which jutted from the point. "Jo."

"Yah."

"Are you noticing these things in the water?" She looked

down and saw the bits of leaves and bark, a few twigs, and over to the left a half empty bottle, pushing half-heartedly against the current. "Oh, oh," she thought half aloud, "can you see what it is?"

"Yes," Ann replied as the bow cleared the point. The view opening before them preceded Ann's explanation. A huge oak had fallen across the river; its roots had been undermined by the land thieving current. Several small trees, broads, crates, an old tire here and there, the remains of a floating dock, and clumps of mud, twigs, and leaves patched the broken limbs to form an impenetrable wall.

"Hold water, Ann!" Jo called as the canoe slid forward with the current. With a quick pull-to stroke, she maneuvered the canoe broadside against the log. The branches held it firm and it sat calmly as the water rushed underneath. "Whew, glad we didn't smash that bow again or you'd be sitting in the water!" Jo sounded relieved but amused at the thought. Ann smiled back as she rested her paddle in front of her, "I don't think that's so funny. Wait till you paddle bow tomorrow."

"Can you reach the machete?"

"Almost, wait a minute," Ann crawled gingerly back over the bedrolls and grasped the machete handle. She handed it back to Jo and watched as she attempted to loosen the branches hanging over a slight gap in the wall. Only a few small ones gave way.

"Don't think we can make it, do you?"

"I don't know. Let me try it." Ann reached for a log and pulled heavily on it but with no success.

"Let's go back and around the other side of the island. That shouldn't be too rough."

"I don't know," Ann paused doubtfully, "it sure looked fast."

"I'm more worried about this current; it's fast enough for trying to buck it upstream," Jo replied, digging her paddle in hard.

"Darn, it won't even budge. Push against the log. That ought to do it. Oops... hold water; oh well, let's try and wade it out."

"Gosh the water's cold. My legs are numb, are yours?"

"Yeh, but my feet are bothering me more. Hold on to 'er a minute while I get my tennies. I can't stand this squishy mud."

"I'm just waiting for you to step on a snake."

"Yeah, well thanks but no thanks, unless of course, you like retrieving upside down canoes."

"Very funny, hurry up would you, I'm freezing."

"Okay climb back in while I steady the canoe. We can surely make it from here." Jo held the canoe tightly as Ann climbed in and hastily pulled her sweatshirt over her bathing suit.

She pushed the canoe on out into the downstream current

and vaulted in. They both fought the current with fast heavy strokes until the threat of being submerged along the left bank was over.

"White water ahead," Ann called back, "I can see it. Oh, never mind, just riffles."

The canoe bobbed through them gently and eased out onto the smooth water.

"That island surely was big, this really seems like a lot of water now that it's all back together," Jo said, relaxing a bit as she pulled her jacket on.

"Was that island on the map? Maybe we can tell how far it is to the Walhonding?"

"Wait a minute, I'll check. No, this road map doesn't show much. I don't see how it can be much farther though. Let's try to camp there, no matter what. I'm so tired, I can hardly believe it." Ann's wary strokes punctuated her sentence.

"Walhonding, that's a pretty name," Jo mused.

"Must be Indian," Ann added sleepily.

"Figures, this is the Black Fork of the Mohican, it leads into the Walhonding and forms the Muskingum, all Indian names."

"Uh, huh," Ann's interest in river names and rivers in general was lagging a bit behind her interest in sleeping.

The shadows were long across the river and the coolness of the shade was chilly and distinct. As the canoe slid from shadow patch to sunlight and back into the dimness again, the warmth of the sun had lost its lingering power.

"I'm about ready to sleep in the canoe. Anything would be better than that stinking mud. This flood must have been a terror. Look at the mud over the bank; I'll bet we couldn't get up it in a hundred years," Ann's voice reflected her disgust.

"I don't much think I care to. It doesn't look too inviting." The bloated carcass of a groundhog floated listlessly along the shore, occasionally other bodies of small animals drowned in their homes could be seen on the mud flats where the water had receded. "No thanks," Jo reaffirmed as she watched the groundhog turn in the water.

The river wound on, increasing its speed steadily but imperceptibly to the two sleepy girls.

"Don't' you think this is dangerous, paddling when it's so dark I mean?" Ann asked plaintively.

"If you happen to see a riverside motel let me know and I'll pull up."

Okay, okay so there's nothing else we can do. I just thought I'd mention it."

"Seriously, have you even seen a tree close enough to the river so we could tie up?"

"No, this must have all been farmland before the flood."

The river twisted around a bend and was swallowed by steep cliffs on either side.

"You think those mud banks were bad. How'd you like to climb these, Chippie?"

Ann smiled at her nickname and puffed out her cheeks. "You think I look like a chipmunk, huh, Pug."

The friendly banter eased off as the last light of the sun disappeared behind the cliff.

"Boy, it's really dark now. What are we going to do?" Ann's smile faded as she looked straight up to the last tinges of gold on the pine at the top of the cliff.

"There's a tree we can tie to. How long's that bow rope?"

"Your humor gets funnier by the hour. I can hardly wait till midnight when you turn back into Charles Adams. Honestly, aren't you worried?"

"Shh! Quiet! Course I am but I'm keeping it a secret and myself might overhear if you're not quiet."

"I think you're getting punchy," Ann tossed back over her shoulder as began stroking again.

"Do you hear a roaring sound, Ann?"

"Yep, Niagara Falls, dead ahead. Says so right here on the map."

"Now who's being ridiculous. Can't you hear it?" For the first time the anxiety in Jo's voice matched Ann's.

"Sure, but it doesn't sound like rapids. It's probably just the wind in the trees, or maybe a freight train. We aren't that far from civilization you know. There's nothing on the map 'till we get to the Muskingum. Haven't see the Walhonding come tripping in anywhere, have you?"

"Oh, well, at least the cliffs are ending. This water is sure in a hurry to get out of here. We're really traveling. Doggone that noise is getting louder. Any bright ideas?"

The canoe hurled out of the gorge before Ann had a chance to answer. Her words changed to a scream as the reality of what faced them sunk into her eyes, accompanied by the roar of her ears.

"Good God," breathed Jo, as she dug her paddle into the water. It was swept from under her grasp as swiftly as if she had been paddling with a broom. "Ann!" she shouted over the roar, "back water, back water, for God's sake!"

Ann snapped from her momentary inertia to a frenzied paddling. She stared at the paddle moving helplessly through the water, refusing to look up again. She had looked for a frozen moment with terror at the gaping dam gate open before her. The image of the steel bars and narrow opening clung to her mind. She'd never needed a second look to remember.

A log pole bumped past them, denting the side of the canoe. The canoe was carried along like a leaf, closer and closer, faster and faster, until Jo dug her paddle in up to her elbow and shut her eyes so tightly they hurt. The rushing was horrible until suddenly it stopped. Ann fell heavily forward onto the cold aluminum of the bow. She grabbed instinctively

for her paddle and caught a
glimpse of the yellow blade dip-
ping into the dark cement tun-
nel.

It took a full second for
them to realize that the canoe was resting gingerly against a
log pole which had wedged cross ways on the opening. "Thank
God, thank you," Jo whispered as she carefully edged the stern
against the cement of the dam. They pulled at the concrete and
the roughness scraped until their knuckles bled, but they
didn't feel it then.

Impulse

The buzzing of the alarm irritated him, but he was too sleepy to roll over and shut it off. He lapsed back into the warmth of the blankets as the buzz faded. Suddenly he sat up as the second alarm went off. It continued ringing until he stumbled over it. "6:30: what an ungodly hour!"

He was still mumbling about it being above and beyond the call of duty as he settled gingerly against the coldness of the chair. He flipped through a few pages of the book he had laid out last night, then turned to his assignment sheet. "Three hundred more pages," he moaned as he leafed through the chapter, *Theories of Reality, Objections to Metaphysics.*

He read steadily; he was thoroughly absorbed in his work and by 7:30 he had covered 50 pages. He glanced up and turned his chair a bit more to the left. The sun was coming through the window now and he paused to admire the violet and red of the little prisms as they fell across the floor. He stared into them for a moment and he felt he was looking at the stained glass window of the little chapel at home, the one with such brilliant reds and blues where Jesus is holding a white lamb in his arm.

He shook his head to clear it of the image and looked back at his book. He read three paragraphs before he realized he'd already covered it, and his eyes skipped angrily down the page until they located his place. He glanced at his watch again, 7:40. He'd covered four more pages in all that time. "Got to keep at it," he glanced again at the slip of newsprint on the wall above his desk. A heavy red pencil encircled the words, "Monday, 8-12 a.m., Philosophy 27 final." The rest of the paper was marked with four other red circles but this was the only one that caught his eye.

He managed to concentrate again and his eyes went rapidly from line to line. A ringing in his ears distracted him, but he managed to ignore it and read a few more pages. Finally he recognized the sound of church bells down the street. He looked at his watch hurriedly, 8 o'clock. He stretched and walked over to shut the window but he couldn't shut out the pealing bells. He settled down again but he wasn't able to read the first line without losing the train of thought. He rose abruptly and flicked on the radio. He turned it from its usual place to a good pop music station. "That ought to take my mind off everything," he mused, "can't possibly think with that rock and roll blaring."

The radio sputtered as it warmed up. "And now friends, the Gospel choir will sing *Jesus Loves Me...*" He clicked it off as the first note of the organ sounded.

"Hell, this is ridiculous. I've got to study somehow."

He sat down on the edge of the bed. He could scarcely believe that weeks and months had gone by so quickly. One day faded into another and then a week was gone.

At home a week could never slip by unnoticed. At least Sundays stood out as a special day, even in the summer, but here every day was the same. Every day was a race against time and an argument between studying and sleeping or occasionally dancing on the weekends. He thought back to the beginning of the quarter when his mom had warned him about this. He had laughed at her then, but here he was caught in a routine that excluded so many things he had felt were important before. He just didn't have time now, he argued with himself. Next week he always promised, when this paper's finished, or this book's read, or this test's over, or...

But it had been three months now and next week never

came. Somehow the old thoughts and beliefs didn't seem so important now, but he could never explain that to Mom. He had learned so many new ideas. He was even ashamed to say what he believed when they argued about Plato's supreme good last week. What he was about to say suddenly seemed so unsophisticated. He didn't intend to make a fool of himself again.

He smoothed the edge of the brown coverlet and stared at it. He reached impulsively for the small black book on the stand near his bed. He brushed at the fingerprints his hands left on the dust of the smoothly grained leather. He let the book fall open and began to read haphazardly, "Ye who do truly and earnestly repent you of your sins... and intend to lead a new life, following the commandments of God, and walking from henceforth in His holy ways; Draw near with faith, and take his holy Sacrament to your comfort..."

He stood up and looked at the alarm clock, 8:45. He could still make it to the 9:15 service. As he hurriedly whipped his black tie into a knot he remembered snatches of a favorite prayer he thought forgotten. "Father of lights... who has kindled in our hearts the desire to know; we bless thee for leading us into a life wherein light and darkness are so wonderfully mingled. On our knees we would learn to think, standing on our feet we would learn to pray... cleanse our prayers with the sanctity of reason, ennoble our reasonings with the mystery of prayer..."

He gave his tie a final pull, grabbed his suit coat and bolted out the door.

The Hunt

$\mathcal{T}$he mountain towered above the road like a painting I'd seen. Yet this one couldn't be canvas; I knew it was real. Still, it was so beautiful. It didn't seem real. The aspen patchwork crisscrossed gray with green. The blue, blue sky was too intense to be a backdrop for the mountain. It forced the green and gray to accept its domination. The white clouds were tied by broken yet gleaming white bond to the new fallen snow that lay under and on the sage and the pine. Their kinship was broken and renewed, broken and renewed, by gray green shrub and towering pine, flecked with their fluffs of snow. The black, sleek Angus, not yet like furry bears, punctuated the lightness of the landscape.

We turned off the main highway and paused by the pole gate. Seconds later we eased the car across the puddles of melting snow and up the muddy hill. As we reached the top, I rolled down my window to feel the cool air. It smelled of clean snow and slightly of sage and freshness. I looked at the pole buildings below and the tingle that shivered through me couldn't be blamed on the cool air. It still seemed hard to believe even after three years. This was the real thing. I was living it here in the West, no longer having to be content with a ranch tucked away on my bookshelf in Ohio, no longer depending on *My Friend Flicka* or Roy Rogers for a glimpse of the life I dreamed of. We slid down the hill, much muddier where the sun had hit it, and paused again before another gate. A long lean black horse gazed down his Roman nose at us as we drove up to the ranch house.

They talked and I thought they'd never finish so we could go. Finally, the horses were caught. Slim, the lanky black horse, eyed me cautiously. The log stable was dripping wet. Overhead bits of the grass roof stuck through the logs. The damp, dripping stable seemed determined to hold on to the last bits of melting snow. Outside the bright sun gobble up as much as she could, but the thick logs and wet roof held her powerless in the barn.

The leather of my saddle smelled good to me. It had been a long four months since I'd last eased into the quilted seat. The softness of my latigo reins were suddenly as familiar again as my leather purse had been all summer. The rifle scabbard under my right leg felt new and strange though; but it too, was exciting. The other horse whirled as his rider mounted. He whirled again and again, around and around. His rider struck him on the side of the head, but still, he whirled and reared. He struck him again, then we moved forward. The horse, Badger, winced as his left eye quivered shut and oozed big tears down his dusky cheek.

We followed the brown ridges of the jeep road which showed muddy humps under the melting snow. We went across the little dam, through an open gate and up toward the groves of "quakies." As we passed another pond on the other side of the fence, six ducks rose in protest. The whirr of their wings and two irritated squawks competed with the rapid but muffled sounds of trotting hoofs. We slowed to a walk as we entered the aspens. Their white barks suddenly reminded me of canoe trips in Michigan and birchbark camp postcards in New York and walks along the French River in Canada. The muffled squish of the melting snow turned to a quiet crunching as we pressed farther into the shade of the grove. The little round leaves looked warm in their snow pockets below us. They had peppered the ground with polka dots of gray and yellow and green, falling before the reds had a chance to appear. We emerged from the woods and crossed the snow of a treeless path. I glanced down and the silent view made the world stand still a moment. For a brief second I joined the air as it filled the space between the snowy hill and the darkness of the wooded valley. We rose again far in the distance to reach the blue gray mountains and gleaming white peaks. But we returned, and Nature left me again on Slim as he made his way back down into the valley. Slim acknowledged my return with shaking of his mane as he felt my contact with his mouth. I found this silence of my interlude broken by the roar of a freight train blowing through the jack pine. We started back down the edge of another grove of "quakies." Fresh tracks crossed before us, and we turned into the timber. The trees seemed to rush at my knee held at an angle by the scabbard. We wound between trees, over logs, and finally up a little rise. Badger's round hips stopped abruptly under Slim's nose. His rider was off in an instant. I tugged at the wooden stock, but the gun wouldn't budge. Two deer raised their heads and then bounded into the trees. The buck, his rack partially hidden in the branches, was halted by his curiosity for a near fatal moment, but he leaped to cover in time. Thank God!

My ankle throbbed a bit, and my knee was stiff from the battle which my leg was waging with the scabbard for possession of the right stirrup. I finally admitted defeat and relinquished the 30-30. Badger danced sideways as his rider buckled the scabbard to his saddle. We wound on through the trees, coming to a fence we backtracked in search of a gate. Finally, a telltale crossing of wire revealed one below us. It was getting dark under the trees, and riding on the edge of the woods was brighter. The wind was coming up, and for the first time I began to feel the chill the sun was leaving behind her.

The clouds were streaked with red and pink. The brilliant sky had to give up its domination of the mountain and become a blueish gray, no more commanding than the mountain's colors.

I buried my nose downward and breathed into the warmth of my wool scarf. My breath felt moist but warm, and the wool had a tantalizing scent of something remembered but not recognized. I raised my head, enjoying the brief moment that my warmed nose held its own against the cold wind, when suddenly the sliver of silver moon, one star and white snow appeared as if they'd just been created before my eyes. They lay pillowed in their blanket of blue-black like silver coins on a rich velvet museum display. The cold and wind cut into my jacket and my Levi's, penetrating all three layers of sweaters, and settling down into my boots paying no need at all to my heavy socks. I shivered and tried to think of other things, but my mind circuited all thoughts and returned to dwell on the pain of the coldness. I wanted to chatter and talk about what we'd seen and done but I knew hunting trips must be silent, so I said nothing. I tried to think of the last time I'd been warm, and then I searched for memories of when I'd been really uncomfortable with heat. My mind wandered only for a minute before remembering that day in Rome.

We awoke early in the morning to find our hotel room hot and stuffy. We had little appetite for breakfast. The streetcar was crowded and hot; it smelled of a mixture of many peoples. Finally, we could stand the pushing and closeness no longer and got off and walked the rest of the way to the coliseum. The sunlight glared on the stones and the cats sunned themselves in the warm air. There must have been 30 of the creatures sharing the ancient seats of Roman emperors. A black cat walked in front of us with all the pride of Nero. I tried for a picture, but she escaped into a shadow.

The welcome breeze at the top of the rows upon rows of the coliseum was but a brief respite from the heat. We were met by a red-hot oven as we stepped out of the cool shade of the huge stone arches. We walked back up to the Forum and after a heated climb, rested a moment on top of Palatine Hill. The heat shimmered about the ruined temples and pools below us. We descended into the baking atmosphere again and walked from shade patch to shade patch until we returned again to the Victor Immanuel monument. The click of my camera was strangely noticeable to me in the roar of traffic all about us. We walked slowly on to the Pantheon and took pictures inside with the sunlight streaming through the huge circular hole in the roof. I caught a good shot of Marty standing in the round pattern of light. We were warm and irritated and then lost in a dirty section of Rome as we attempted to decipher the Italian street names and correlate them with the English on our map.

We looked sufficiently bewildered for a kindly Italian gentleman to come up and nod his head in the direction of a short narrow street before us, saying, "Trevi Fountain is that way." The cool sound of the water and the excitement of seeing the fountain revived us a bit, and we sought directions to the Spanish Steps. The climb up the Steps was unbelievable; the heat radiated about our feet; we were so hot and miserable but there was no sense in turning back. I sincerely doubted if I could keep putting one foot in front of the other much longer, but we finally made it to the cool shade of the park at the top. We sank into the funny little low benches and began to attempt eating our sack lunches. It's a frustrating situation to be hungry yet too warm and tired to eat. We made our way to an overlook high above the crowded streets. Far to our left Victor Immanuel stuck out like a white elephant and nearly directly ahead of us, Saint Peter's with our hotel concealed in front of it, was visible many, many blocks away. The Tiber wound between our two points of travel with its inviting but dirty water. We slanted down the road with its switchbacks until we eventually reached the hot dusty street level. We somehow managed to arrive on the right bank of the Tiber rather than on the street to Saint Peter's but the water gave at least a suggestion of being cool and refreshing as we followed it. Stopping for our fifth treat of "Gelati" for the day we sank down beside the walled riverbank. The ice cream slid down our throats with about the same amount of energy as the little Italian boys sliding into the Tiber below us and floating lazily with the current to the next bridge. At last, we came to Hadrian's Tomb, and realized, with the emptiness of the relief that comes solely from a very tiring experience, that we had only a few more blocks to go.

The jolt of Slim's initial attempts to start into a trot quickly transported me the thousands of miles from Rome to Colorado. Unfortunately, the Italian heat wave stayed behind, and my nose and feet were numb from the jabbing cold. I first tried to sit to the trot and then bounce in an attempt to get warm. This was partially successful, but my mind soon wandered to other desires. The steady rhythm of broad shoulders rising and falling while posting to Bader's short-gaited trot was barely distinguishable ahead of me in the darkness. I thought immediately of how warm it would be to curl up and lay my head on that shoulder; I thought of how the coldness would disappear in the warmth of sleep, and love.

I blinked unbelievingly at the small light coming from the ranch house window. We were almost there. I began to dread dismounting as I felt in advance the needles of pain shooting through my feet as they first touched the ground. I hobbled from the corral into the warm circle of heat issuing from the old wood burning stove. The coffee smelled inviting on the stove but tasted bitter in my mouth. With my boots and shoes removed my feet began to thaw little by little. As the hunting talk began, I returned to Rome.

Anticipation

The headlights flashed in the mirror above the mantle. Gail watched the car closely as it rounded the corner. She looked back to her book as she discerned the smooth outline of a Lincoln. She got up and walked to the open door. The rain bounced into little circles under the streetlight. She pressed her nose against the moist screen and felt the warmth of the late summer night as it still withstood the cooling rain. Another car came slowly down the street, and she peered hard into the dark as it left the range of the far streetlight. She sighed and turned away when it disappeared. She walked back to the chair but ignored her book and picked up the mag again. "Surely, he must at least be in the State by now," she mused half aloud. The big red Setter at her feet looked up but lolled his head back on the rug and merely stretched in answer. She had been tracing his probable route and stopping places since Thursday now. Two days and twelve hours later he was seven hours overdue. "Maybe it's the rain... could be raining harder west of here." The Setter again raised his head, this time far enough to lick her ankle. She patted him gently and then ruffled the fur over his ribs. She walked back to the door and listened to his soft paws change to a click as he followed her from the carpeted living room to the tile of the entry way. "Poor fellow," she took his big jaws in her hands and pressed his head against her cheek, "you know, don't you? Just one suitcase makes a shadow out of you. All these bags and boxes of mine must really worry you."

"Darling, please come into bed. There's no sense waiting up all night." Her mother's voice was quiet, but it woke her from her momentary daze.

"Okay, don't push it; I'm a big girl now." She laughed casually but her mother didn't return her smile. Twenty-one years weren't enough to convince either of them.

Gail stifled a yawn and crawled off the couch. She walked slowly to the door and watched rain drizzle halfheartedly down. She glanced at her watch. 12:35. Time was passing about normally, she decided, but her desires were racing far ahead as they had been doing the last three months.

The street was quiet. Cars rarely passed now. She glanced from the glaring streetlight to the misty darkness of the woods across the road. They hadn't changed much. Perhaps twelve years weren't many to the pines but so many to her. The first time she remembered seeing the woods, she mused as she returned to the couch, she had vowed then and there that someday, somehow, she would be riding a horse, a big black Arabian stallion, over those intriguing paths and across the fieldstone bridges. Amazingly enough, she thought, it had come true. Although the horse wasn't a flashy black stallion (he was only a gray, chubby, ex-lead pony for Calumet stables) the woods had been every bit as exciting as she'd imagined. Her mind ran back over the first exploratory rides. The day she and Adelle had discovered the limestone falls, and then the time they turned onto a new path and there was a deserted sawmill right before them and some months later they found the spot where a tree had been blown down and Misty and Holly had loved to eat the dirt there so. They'd head for it whenever they crossed the border from Black's estate into Vincents'.

She smiled as she thought of the time Holly spun around the jump in the jump lane they'd built in the upper woods and then as she spun, she sat down and they both had been so amazed. Holly was embarrassed for an hour after that. Gail nearly giggled aloud as she remembered how comical and embarrassed horses could be. The time Misty turned sharply to the right at the forks where they always went left wasn't so funny though... it was her first day riding bareback out in the woods. She was proud of how well she had been staying on. That's probably why he did it. But she had tumbled head over heels, straight ahead as he cantered on around the corner. Adelle had laughed a lot. But she had laughed back the next week when Adelle decided to play Tarzan and lifted herself out of the saddle on a grapevine which hung down in the trail. It startled poor Holly and they spent an hour catching her. Couldn't blame the poor horse though, since...

A pair of lights lit up the street before her as a car came slowly around from the west side of the house. This immediately broke into her reverie, and she jumped to the door only to see the car pull into Herrin's drive. Rogue thrust his cold nose into her hand. "Poor pup," she murmured. She pulled one long silky ear gently and tickled under his chin.

She couldn't seem to remember what she had been think-ing of but looking up at the mirror above the mantle, she was reminded of the mirrors in the big riding hall. It had always been so exciting to trot there over the frozen winter country-side. The warm hall and tanbark were a world away from the cold weather outside, and she and Adelle had spent hours playing horseshow and drill team. She remembered going there again, but that was much later, only five years ago. She and Rogue had gone to the Black's Riding Arena, as it said in the announcement in *The News Journal*...“every Wednesday night, until they had learned to heel, to sit stay, to stand for examination, recall, do figure eights, and most important, had learned not to wave a tail or bark a friendly greeting in the middle of a demonstration.”

She looked down at Rogue's beautiful head and remembered how they had burst with Irish pride when she had pinned the second-place ribbon on his collar. His paws were twitching now, perhaps dreaming of the walks they had taken this week among the birches in the woods. She loved those birches. It was her favorite spot in the whole woods. They were rather rare in Ohio, and this seemed to make them all the more graceful and pure. There had been birch trees farther down too, a mile or so away where they used to jump the hedge which lined the road. They were gone now. Dr. Dewald's new brick house sat right where they'd been. It had been meadows, trees, and hedges then. Crazy kids, she thought. She wondered as she remembered vaulting over the hedge and then swerving the horse at the last moment to miss a car coming down the road. That wasn't the craziest thing though. That night in high school when a bunch of the gang swerved their cars into Black's Lane to play, Dave had driven his dad's big station wagon out into the terraced gardens and over a little rock waterfall. She had loved to sit by the stream and watch Mists' nose move in the grass. No, jumping hedges wasn't the stupidest thing she had done.

Another night of her high school life was even more unhappy. It had been wonderful to get home that night. Mom and Dad had met her at the airport in Columbus. She had loved that trip to California for the Rose Bowl game and had had so much to tell about the Buckeyes bringing back the crown for Ohio State. They were nearly home when Dad's voice, talking about the ashes in the air and red glow, awoke her. She sat in silence as they drove through the big gate off Marion Avenue towards the fire. She didn't cry as she watched the riding hall and stables disappear into the redness against the night. She just watched and petted Captain's inky nose. It was kind of Cliff to let her hold him. It helped a lot. He was so pretty – the only true black horse she'd ever seen. Wonder if he's still alive; probably not, he must be at least...

A car stopped before the house. She jumped to the door and ran out into the rain. The moment and those to come swallowed up Black's Wood more completely than the dark. She didn't hear the whisper of the pine as dashed to the car, but they had nothing to say to her now.

An Ode to the Good Death and the Good Doctor

O Puff - O Magical Dragon of a dog,
You of such grace, you with the look of eagles, now so
dimmed,
Now circling, now stumbling, now falling, now unable to rise
Now immobile, now only a wagging tail as we sooth and hold
you
My heart breaking with every beat, our tears falling.

You who gave me so many gifts of devotion and love and the
joy of life,
Now the only gift we can give you is this love and this
Peace at this last kiss.

    Your euthanasia shall have to be a kind of healing,
    The only healing we can offer now, each grateful for the
    ease of it.

    Peace, Beloved; Peace: ease from the suffering,
    Ease off to your new green meadows and sparkling
    streams; romp with joy and love.

    Life - it goes on; go with it again, conquering, striding,
    Magical Puff, you of such grace and beauty, leaving
    behind only this empty, graying shell fading away into
    the leaping greenly spirits of trees.

    But... tarry there - wait a heartbeat - there in your new
    paradise and we'll meet again, halfway across the sky in
    our dreams.

    Farewell. Fare well.

About the Author

Virginia Joyann "Jody" Haley Smith was born April 2, 1938 in Toledo, Ohio. At the age of 83, Jody passed away May 9, 2021. She was the daughter of the late Peter Franklin and the late Virginia Wurl (Rhonemus) Haley, sister of the late Dr. Gary Haley DDS. Jody was a 1956 graduate of Mansfield High School, Mansfield, Ohio, and received her Bachelor of Science and Arts, majoring in English, from Colorado A&M (now Colorado State) in 1960. Jody was a member and served as chaplain of her sorority, Tri Delta, member of Phi Delta Epsilon (National Honorary Journalism Fraternity), Phi Kappa Phi (National Honorary Scholastic Society) and Lambda Iota Tau (Literature Honorary). Jody was a member of the Aggie All-Girl Mounted Quadrille precision riding team, president of the French Club and served as an editor for *The Collegian*. At Colorado A&M, she met the love of her life, the late Abbott Pliny "Pete" Smith III DVM. They married on September 4, 1959. In 1963, Pete and Jody moved to Ohio establishing Milliron Farm, eventually opening Milliron Veterinary Clinic. Knowing Athens was the place they would spend their lives, added stability for the Smith family to grow and be of service to their community. Jody is remembered fondly by her grandchildren as a strong-willed woman who taught them many life lessons, including farm life – passing on her love of animals, rescuing many from danger. Jody's love for horses, all animals, served her well as a veterinarian's wife. Her many accolades included winning the 1976 AKC National Specialty Best of Winners with her beloved Belgian Sheepdog, The Magic Dragon V Siegestor CD/TD, "Puff". "All things in moderation" and "No thank you helpings" were her constant refrain with her children and grandchildren.

Other Books in this Series:

Milliron: Abbott "Pete" Smith D.V.M.: The Biography
Tails of a Country Vet I
Tails of a Country Vet II
The South High Horseman

www.ingramcontent.com/pod-product-compliance
Lightning Source LLC
Chambersburg PA
CBHW071411170626
46811CB00003B/1351